How the birds got their colours

Told by
Mary Albert

Retold and illustrated by
Pamela Lofts

MAD
HATTER
BOOKS

Slawson Communications, Inc.
San Diego, CA 92103-4316

This is the story
of how the birds
got their colours.

Long, long ago – in the Dreamtime –

when the land and animals were being made . . .

. . . all the birds were black —
all one colour.   Till . . .

. . . one day,
a little dove flew around
looking for food.

He flew down to the ground
to catch a big juicy grub.

But instead, he landed
right on a sharp stick!

It pierced his little foot
and made him very sick.

For days, he lay on the ground in pain.
His foot swelled up.

He was dying!

All his mates gathered around
to see how they could help.

All except crow.

He just wandered around
with his hands behind his back.

Suddenly,
the parrot rushed forward —
and with her sharp beak . . .

burst

the little dove's swollen foot!

Colour splashed out all over the parrot.
Red and green and blue ran down
her chest, wings and tail.

It splashed out all over the other birds.
Some got red, some brown,
some blue, some yellow.

Some got spots.

Some got stripes.

All got colours.

All except crow, who was standing
away from the others.

Crow got no colour at all!

So that's how the birds got their colours.

And as for the dove,
he soon got better,
thanked the parrot . . .

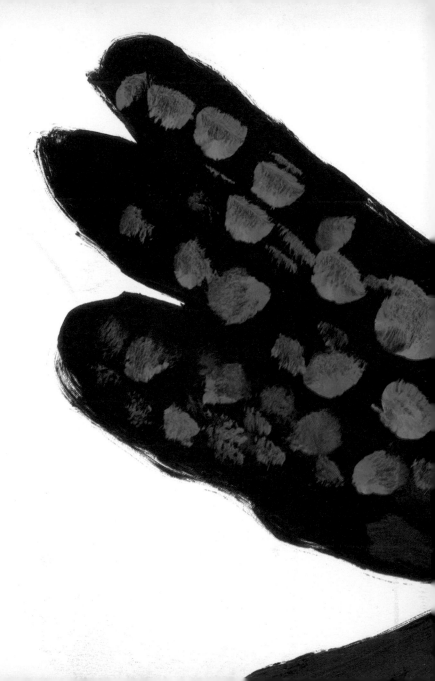

and was able to fly away.